Katje
the Windmill Cat

Gretchen Woelfle

ILLUSTRATED BY Nicola Bayley

CANDLEWICK PRESS
CAMBRIDGE, MASSACHUSETTS

Katje had an easy life.
She lived with Nico the miller in a Dutch village by the sea.
While Nico ground grain in his windmill, Katje chased
mice. Up and down the ladders she prowled, searching behind
sacks of grain and along beams dusty with flour.

"Every miller needs a cat like Katje," Nico told the villagers who
came to buy his flour.

At night Katje slept on a soft pillow beside Nico.

On Sundays they walked along the dike that protected the village
from the sea. Katje chased seagulls. Nico watched for storms.

One morning Nico didn't follow Katje to the mill. He put on his best suit and walked to town. In the evening he came back with a young woman on his arm. She wore a fine dress and carried a bouquet of flowers. Nico carried a bright copper kettle, a bundle of dresses, and a brand-new broom.

"It's a plain house, Lena," Nico said shyly.

"It's perfect," Lena said. "Just right for a miller and his wife."

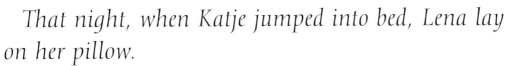

That night, when Katje jumped into bed, Lena lay
on her pillow.

"Meow," whined Katje.

Nico picked her up. "Run along, Katje."

"Meow," insisted Katje.

Nico closed the curtains around the bed.

"Meow," complained Katje even louder. The curtains
remained closed and Katje slept in the kitchen.

The next day Lena
began to sweep.
She swept the house.
She swept the path
to the mill. She even
swept flour dust from
Nico when he came
home at night.

"Take off your
wooden shoes
before you walk
in the house,"
Lena scolded.

Nico stepped out of his shoes and kissed her. He left a big white smudge on her cheek.

Katje crept past them. She wouldn't let Lena sweep her. But Katje left a trail of white paw prints and Lena saw them.

"Shoo, Katje," she cried. "You're too dusty."

Life wasn't easy anymore.

One day Katje woke to the sound of sawing.

"I'm making a cradle," Nico said.

Lena laid a soft quilt inside. That night Katje jumped in the cradle and curled up on the quilt.

Soon a baby called Anneke was born in the little house by the windmill. She was small and pink, and she slept in the cradle. Katje didn't mind. There was room enough for both of them.

But Lena said, "Shoo, Katje. You'll make Anneke sneeze."

Katje played with Anneke when Lena wasn't looking. Katje batted the ribbons on the cradle. Anneke waved her arms.

Katje wriggled under the quilt. Anneke kicked her legs.

Katje jumped from side to side and set the cradle rocking. Anneke giggled and Katje meowed.

This was more fun than chasing mice.

But when Lena heard them she said, "Shoo, Katje. You'll tip over the cradle!"

Katje walked across the room and stopped by the door. Lena didn't call her back.

So Katje left the house and moved to the windmill.

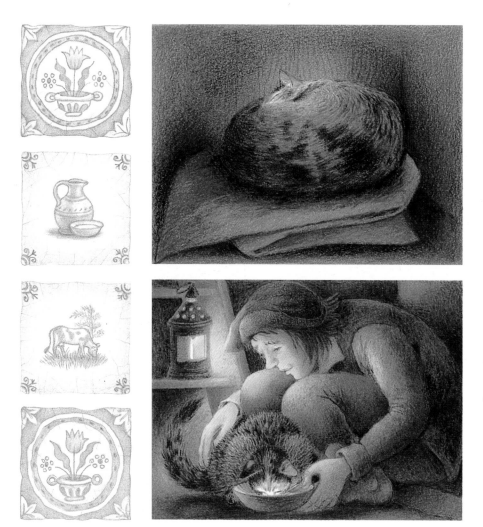

At night she curled
up on empty flour sacks
and dreamed of soft quilts.
Nico brought her a dish of
milk every evening.

"Come home, Katje.
We miss you."

Katje wouldn't go home
with Nico. But sometimes,
when everyone was sleeping,
she crept back home and
gently rocked the cradle
while Anneke slept.

One afternoon dark clouds gathered overhead. The wind howled and rain pounded against the windmill.

"We've been through many storms, haven't we?" Nico said, scratching Katje's head.

Katje purred.

The windmill sails whirled, and the great millstones turned.

"I won't have a minute's rest till the wind dies down," Nico said. He had to keep grinding the grain between the millstones. If the stones rubbed together, the sparks could start a fire.

Katje rubbed against Nico's leg. She would work as long as he did.

Nico hoisted heavy bags of grain to the top of the mill and watched the wheat pour down to the millstones. Katje ran up and down the ladder, and round and round the mill. She looked for mice who might sneak in from the storm.

All night long the wind roared, the windmill shook, and the millstones groaned.

When morning finally came, the door flew open and Lena came in with a basket of bread and herring for Nico's breakfast.

Katje dashed to the house to see Anneke.

A crowd of villagers ran down the road. "The dike has broken! The sea is flooding the town!" Church bells clanged. Water rushed into the house. Katje jumped on Anneke's cradle.

Lena and Nico waded out of the mill as the cradle swept out of the house. "Anneke!" cried Lena.

"I'll get the rowboat!" yelled Nico.

Katje and Anneke raced through the flooded streets. Furniture, wagons, and even houses swirled by.

Some villagers stood on rooftops. Others climbed up the dike.

"There's a cradle!"

"I pray there's no baby in it!"

"It's sure to capsize!"

A wagon wheel whirled past and sent the cradle spinning.

"Look, there's Katje!"

"It's Anneke's cradle!"

The cradle tipped back and forth. But Katje jumped from side to side and kept Anneke safe.

Finally the cradle bumped against the dike. The rowboat bumped next to it.

"Dear Anneke!" cried Nico as he plucked her from the cradle.

"Darling Katje!" cried Lena, hugging her tightly.

"Meow," said Katje.

Anneke soon grew too big for her cradle, so Katje slept there on a soft quilt that Lena made just for her.

Katje had a busy life. In the morning she played with Anneke. All day she chased mice in the windmill. And when she came home at night, she always remembered to lick her paws before she stepped into the house. ❧

ON NOVEMBER 5, 1421, ST. ELIZABETH'S DAY a violent storm blew in from the North Sea, breaking through the dikes and flooding a small village in South Holland. *Katje, the Windmill Cat* is based on a true story of the Elizabeth's Day Flood. A cat and a little baby did live through that terrible flood.

After the storm, the villagers built a bigger, stronger dike to hold back the sea. They moved their houses and the windmill to the top of the dike, so the village would never be flooded again. The villagers named the new dike the Kinderdijk—which means Children's Dike in Dutch— to honor the baby who was saved by the brave cat.

Today, nineteen windmills still line the Kinderdijk. Tourists can ride down the canal alongside the windmills and go inside to see how they work.

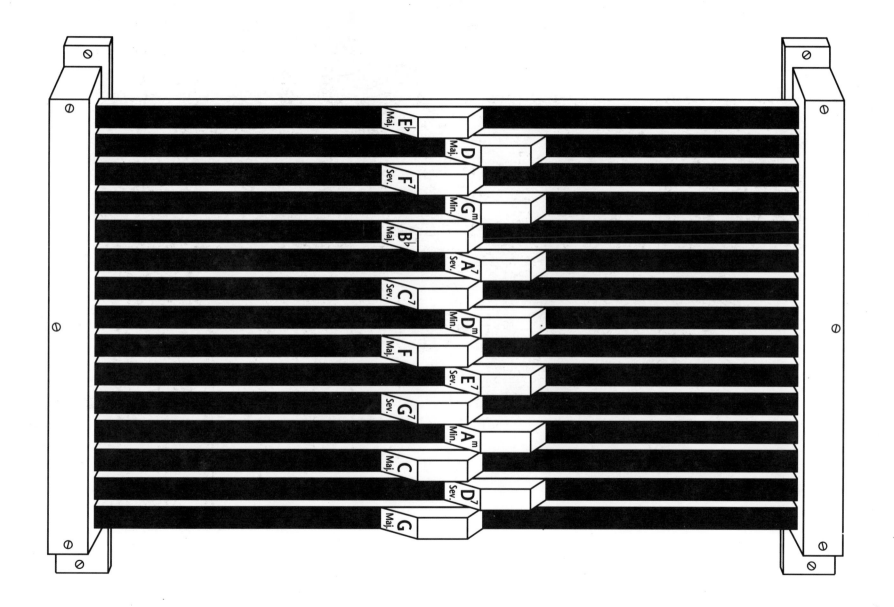